Nowhere to Be Found

ALSO BY BAE SUAH

Highway with Green Apples

Nowhere to Be Found

Bae Suah

Translated by Sora Kim-Russell

amazoncrossing

Text copyright © 1998 Bae Suah
Translation copyright © 2015 Sora Kim-Russell
All rights reserved.

Previously published by Jakkajungsin in Korea in 1998. Translated from Korean by Sora Kim-Russell. First published in English by AmazonCrossing in 2015.

Published by AmazonCrossing, Seattle

www.apub.com

Amazon, the Amazon logo, and AmazonCrossing are trademarks of Amazon.com, Inc., or its affiliates.

ISBN-13: 9781477827550
ISBN-10: 1477827552

Cover design by David Drummond

Library of Congress Control Number: 2014919162

Printed in the United States of America

In 1988 I was temping at a university in Gyeonggi Province.

Mostly what I did there was send lecture requests to part-time instructors, make adjustments to their class schedules, mail them their pay stubs, and field complaints from students. As far as the work went, I didn't have any major complaints of my own. It was the kind of clerical work that anyone could have done without any special qualifications or expertise. As long as you had a decent memory and an elementary work ethic, there was nothing to fear. In other words, it bore no resemblance at all to the type of job you could get only after having studied hard for years and years, turned in thousands upon thousands of pages of reports, written a tome of a thesis, earned a degree, and created a winning résumé composed entirely in English.

At this job we could chew gum or do our nails while answering the phones and take over two hours to type even the sparsest syllabus. We weren't lazy or indifferent or anything. It was just the nature of the work. The office got a lot of visitors, so it wasn't unusual for me to make more than twenty cups of coffee in a single day. Of course, it was muddy instant coffee.

Every person and every procedure marches on at a measured pace. That's how things get done, just as the less delicate components of a machine submit to the will of the machine without any conscious thought or shred of volition while being steadily ground down. So while I was busy not having any conscious thought, I became a cog. The office I worked in was not a place where revolution happens. Nor should it have been. The general ethic there was of loyalty to one's assigned task, whether that meant stirring twenty cups of instant coffee or fielding requests from professors for photocopies, for the purpose of solemnly achieving that ethic itself. Though that applied only to the members of the lower classes, of course. When I put it that way, you might think I'm being cynical, but that's not it. The work didn't bother me—except, of course, for the little things, like having to ride the bus for over an hour to get there and having no hope of ever getting a raise since I was only a temporary contract worker. As for my friends, one was a government bureaucrat, another had just started working at a brokerage firm, and another was teaching in an orphanage, but most were unemployed. It's possible I harbored a vague sense of fear back then.

I didn't have too many tasks, but I also wasn't so idle that I could have passed the time knitting. When I was working, the hours went by at what I can only call a measured pace. My salary was, of course, very small. If not for that, I might have worked there longer. We got a month off while classes were out of session. I spent that month working part-time in a dye factory close to my house. My job was to screw caps onto tubes of dye using a mechanical device. That was a long time ago.

I'm sure that dye factory has since found a more modern solution to that primitive final step of production. But then again, if they had modernized any earlier, I wouldn't have spent that summer wrapped in the suffocating smell of acrylics.

Every now and then I picture a subway train at night packed with people I used to know and random people whom I will meet by chance in some distant future. Most of the people I knew long ago now live their lives without me, and those whom I will meet by chance one day do not know me now. They walk by apathetically, their faces gloomy beneath the dim lights of the city hall subway station, jostling my shoulders as they pass.

If you get off the subway at city hall and walk behind the Plaza Hotel, you'll find the restaurant where I used to work nights after finishing my shift at the university. Inside the old wooden gate, a pine tree twists up out of the yellow soil of the courtyard at uncannily exquisite angles, and a gravel pathway leads you to the building where you must slip off your shoes, step up onto the raised wooden floor, and walk past a row of small rooms hidden behind sliding doors covered in white paper. The whole thing looks shabby and run-down. People go to this restaurant, which squats behind the hotel like an old man, to eat dinner or drink alcohol or to rent one of the private rooms on Friday nights to play poker, and sometimes even to smoke a little marijuana. I washed dishes, served food, mopped the floor, and fetched cigarettes for customers. Sometimes I even earned a thousand-*won* tip.

Tired. I was tired. I was only twenty-four, but I was tired. For a long time I'd been feeling dizzy just from getting up from the toilet. On the bus in the morning, I would doze off while standing, one hand gripping the hanging strap. Dry lips I couldn't hide behind lipstick. Bloodshot eyes and the nausea of an empty stomach. The horror of rough skin, rough tongue.

I'd once dreamt of becoming a veterinarian. It was a dream I'd given up on long ago. In order to make that dream come true, I would've had to go back to college, but that was impossible. I was the only person in my family who was making any money. Our family looked perfect from the outside: a mother, a father, a brother ten years older than me, and a sister ten years younger. I don't know how my parents created such an odd age gap. Even now I think maybe my family is just a random collection of people I knew long ago and will never happen upon again, and people I don't know yet but will meet by chance one day. Their dim, indistinct faces will ultimately, and meaninglessly, become the faces of the people in my life, though at the present moment they are unfamiliar strangers with no influence over me whatsoever. The shoulders of strangers that bump against mine in the subway. The lukewarm touch of a hand proffering a tip in a restaurant. The voice over the phone of a guest lecturer on criminal sociology whose face I've never seen.

"This week's topic is murder."

"Oh."

"Eight o'clock on Saturday night. I'll be lecturing for three hours."

"Will you be using video?"

"No."

"If you do decide to, I'll have to put in an equipment request."

"There's no need. I don't plan on showing any videos. But . . ."

"Yes, go ahead."

"I heard the midterm exam grading sheets were changed."

"That's correct."

"You don't normally mail those out?"

"All of the new forms were mailed to you."

"I didn't receive any."

"I'm certain I mailed them. Aren't you Professor Gang Jin-gu of Kangnam University? They were sent to your office."

"I'm not Professor Gang Jin-gu of Kangnam University. I don't teach at any university. I work for a company and teach part-time at night. You must have me confused with someone else."

My mind went blank for a moment. For the past several months, I had assumed that the person teaching criminal sociology was Professor Gang Jin-gu of Kangnam University, and I had sent that person all sorts of materials and brochures. I had also taken the occasional phone call that I thought was from him. Professor Gang Jin-gu had taught something similar up until last year. I hurriedly rummaged through my files and pulled out the list of instructors. Sure enough, the man on the phone was right. I felt embarrassed.

13

"You're right," I said in a small voice.

"I'm sure it was a simple mistake."

"I'm so sorry. I'll send the forms again."

"It's no big deal."

He seemed like a nice person.

"If you're free on Saturday, would you like to come to my lecture? It'll be an interesting one—"

I cut him off. "What kinds of people commit murder?"

"Murderers, I suppose."

"Why do they do it?"

"I'm sure they have their reasons."

"Is this how all of your lectures go?"

"Of course not. I make it a rule to read directly from the textbook. If I want to confuse the students, I read the chapters in reverse. That keeps them on their toes, since none of them have read to the end yet. It's a simple method but an effective one. So do you think you can come on Saturday?"

"I don't think so. I work nights downtown."

"Every night?"

"Yes, every night."

"What do you do?"

"Dishes and cleaning," I said with a sigh.

There was silence for three seconds.

"You're not serious," he said. "Anyway, I'll take that to mean you can't make it."

If anyone in my family could be described as still incomplete of character that would be my little sister. She was a bony wisp of a girl with a chest that seemed to have stopped in the middle of developing and gangly arms and coltish legs, but among us siblings she had the highest grades in school. Still in middle school, she would amaze my brother and me by using a clever technique to solve simultaneous equations or figuring out perfectly and in less than twenty seconds some type of square root that we'd never seen before. But that was the extent of what I knew about her. We were too far apart in age to really feel like sisters, and we hadn't had much opportunity to spend time together as we were growing up. We'd never shared a room or liked the same boy or fought over a pair of lacy underwear; instead we lived our lives barely aware of each other's existence.

One Sunday afternoon, possibly in the spring of that same year, I woke up late, took a bath, and was

passing through the kitchen to hang my wet towel outside when I heard her crying. I wondered what was
wrong. The first thing that came to mind was that she
must've finally started her period. It was a silly idea. I
had no idea whether she was already menstruating, but
I assumed that was what would make a girl her age cry.
She was too old to be crying over cookies or watercolor
pencils, and too young to be crying over a boy.

"Mia, what's wrong?"

Out of a desire to help my young sister, I told her
it was nothing. She wasn't alone. All girls went through
it. It was a little uncomfortable at first but once she
got used to it, she would hardly notice it at all. It was
just something you had to deal with, no different from
brushing your teeth in the morning or showering. And
so on, and so on.

"I want to go on a class trip."

Her words took me completely by surprise. I would
truly never have guessed that she would want to go on
a trip with her class. I'd certainly never gone on one,
and I can't imagine it was any different for our brother:
school excursions had never been an option for us.
When the other kids went off on trips, I reported to

school and did my homework alone in the empty classroom. I neatly copied hundreds of pages from the Korean textbook into my notebook, solved equations, drew apples on plates, and wiped down the tops of the desks with a damp rag. The leisurely spring or autumn sky would stretch out beyond the windows of that deserted classroom, and the only sound I would hear was a pencil rolling across the floor between the empty seats. For my brother and me, staying behind wasn't that bad.

"Neither of us ever went on a class trip," I told her, not bothering to conceal my surprise. "We didn't think it was that big of a deal."

"This is different. They're going on an airplane. On an *airplane*. All anyone can talk about is this trip. If I don't get to go, my friends will stop talking to me."

Her voice was so firm. Our brother and I had never had any friends—at least not the kinds of friends you wanted to go on a class trip with or hold hands with on the way home from school. When we were in school, we probably wouldn't have been that sad at the thought of being ditched by our friends. But our sister was different. She wanted to braid her hair exactly like the other

17

girls did and fold over her socks exactly as they did. On her birthday or other special days, gifts of cookies and flowers from her friends would show up at our house. Mia had an androgynous charm about her, like Tyltyl in Maeterlinck's *The Blue Bird*, which attracted other girls to her. For all I knew it was an act of cruelty to tell a child like her not to go on a class trip. I couldn't go on any trips because we were too poor, and as for my brother, I'd heard it was because he didn't get along with the other students. Neither he nor I mourned our family's poverty or our maladjustment to the group. Being poor or being lonely could be either fortunate or unfortunate, but the truth is that the distinction was meaningless. Whether we were fortunate or not, we were still different, and that's all there was to it.

"I'll die if I can't go on this trip."

After the years had passed and my little sister was grown up, would she too inherit the cynicism and apathy toward the world that enabled our family line to endure poverty and maladjustment, just as my brother and I had? Maybe, but she hadn't yet.

"I'm getting my paycheck from the restaurant today or tomorrow," I said, stroking her hair. "You can use that to pay for the trip."

"That's your lunch money."

"Doesn't matter. I'll pack my lunch this month."

I didn't tell her that I would most likely be skipping lunch that month since it was hard to wake up early and there was rarely any leftover rice or other food in the fridge.

My brother sometimes came by the restaurant to walk me to the subway after I got off work late at night. One Sunday night we were in the city hall station underpass when the last train was leaving. My body felt heavy, like it was sinking deeper and deeper into the underpass.

"How are you holding up?" he asked.

My brother was a man of few words. Though we lived under the same roof, I rarely heard his voice. He'd once had a job guarding the Blue House, the president's residence. After quitting he'd become one of the many ordinary people who failed at everything they tried to do. He hadn't gone to college, and he wasn't a computer genius.

"I'm a little tired, but it's manageable," I said to him there in the underpass. "At least the restaurant isn't too busy on Sundays."

"Do you have to keep working nights? You barely get any sleep beforc you're up again for your day job."

The worn-down heels of my brother's sneakers descended the stairs. Up until last month he'd had a job as a night watchman on a construction site.

"I'm sorry I can't do more for you," he said.

"You don't have to say that. I'm all right."

"I'm going to Japan. There's work there."

"When?"

"Not sure yet. Maybe as soon as next month."

"What kind of work?"

"A janitorial service in Osaka. If I work hard, I'll be able to save up and not be cheated out of my pay this time."

"What kind of cleaning do they do?"

"Different kinds. Sewers, roads, septic tanks."

"How long will you be gone?"

"For as long as possible. The visa is only good for a year, but if I can't get an extension, I'll stay there illegally if I have to. Once I'm settled, I'll send you money."

"You don't have to do that."

"You're struggling too hard for someone who has an older brother and parents, albeit incompetent ones."

"No. I'm healthy and I went to college, which you didn't even get to do. I'll get by. But what about you?"

My brother was thirty-four years old and still unmarried, though he'd once lived with a woman for about a year until they broke up over money. I sometimes felt bad for him because of that. I was in high school when he broke up with her and moved home. One Saturday afternoon, when the sunlight was turning everything golden, I'd returned home from school and was washing my clothes under the tap in the courtyard. For some reason I turned to look behind me. My brother was standing there. How long had he been watching me? He asked me to go with him to the market. I said I had to finish the laundry, but his voice took on an uncharacteristically crabby tone.

"Just drop it and let's go," he said.

At the market he bought me a plate of *mandu*. Then, to my utter astonishment, he bought me a washing machine. I was so overjoyed that I couldn't stop grinning. A seventeen-year-old girl was so happy about receiving a washing machine that she could have cried. Later I learned that he had used the deposit from the apartment he'd rented with his girlfriend to buy it for me. He left home that night without eating dinner. Each step he took seemed to kick up a breeze.

At some point that same year, Cheolsu joined the army.

He sent me the occasional letter while he was in the service. They were very brief. Most were about clouds or the weather. If boys could be divided into different categories, then Cheolsu was a mineral. That was his approach to life. He was neither dishonest nor dramatic. He wasn't my one and only boyfriend, and I wasn't his one and only girlfriend. He didn't attend lectures on political economy or register for study groups on proletariat literature, but he also wasn't hung up on studying for the civil service exam or professional exams like other people. He just looked blank sometimes. While everyone else was tormented by a restless anxiety, like the dizziness you feel on a spring day, which made them question what they were doing with their lives, Cheolsu was yawning and working on a crossword puzzle. He knew how to accept the tedium without the ennui.

I could count about a dozen or so girls whom Cheolsu had dated back then. His interest in them was closer to simple curiosity than passion. He took them out to dinner and coffee, went with them to the movies, and even joined them at the occasional protest rally or demonstration. But I don't believe that any of it—not the movies or the demonstrations or the jazz concerts at Janus or the French conversation classes at Alliance Française—really moved him. If someone asked him how the movie was that he'd watched with a girl the day before, he would answer, *Okay, I guess. I forgot the title, but it's about a spy. Or maybe a beggar? His woman leaves him or dies or something. I don't know. I fell asleep and missed the ending.* Cheolsu's response never varied, regardless of whether it was a trendy Hollywood movie or a 1960s French film or a live play put on by the Yeonwoo Theater Company. And he always ended with the same words: *I'm not really sure.*

Among the girls he'd dated, one had snow-white skin and eyes that looked good behind glasses. She spent all her time going back and forth between home and the lecture hall, private French lessons, and the French literature section in the library, as if the academic life were the only one worth living. Yet I don't believe she had any particularly grand dreams for herself. She later married an ordinary salaryman (who was not from France) and lived off his wages in Seoul, where she had no use for all that French. Then there was the loud, not-all-that-pretty girl with no sense of feminine wiles who later became a math teacher; the fervent socialist; the intellectual beauty who attended a top private university; the jealous girl; and the girl who was called the Black Hole because of her reputation for routinely going through multiple guys in one night. Each time Cheolsu broke up with another, he said the same thing.

I'm not really sure.

Basic training ended and Cheolsu came home on furlough. He'd changed. I couldn't explain exactly how he'd changed, but his face was tanned as dark as a laborer's and only his eyes sparkled. His hands were rough and he spoke less frequently. Cheolsu sat down next to me with a can of Coke in his hand.

"Why are you so busy all the time?" The first words out of his mouth were a complaint. "You didn't reply to any of my letters."

"I was working."

"Give me your hand."

He stroked my hand. I knew what he wanted. This new Cheolsu didn't waste any time. His lips fumbled their way toward me. It was an emotionless and unthrilling first kiss.

"Want to go back to my place?" he asked.

He'd been to my house several times, but I'd never gone to his. It was too far away, and I knew he lived with his parents and younger sister. I hesitated because I had to work at the restaurant that night, but then said yes because I didn't want to let him down after he'd gotten out on furlough. He took me by the hand and stood up. In the bus on the way to his house, he sat me on his lap and stared into my eyes. I stroked his closely cropped hair. The gray landscape outside the window flowed past listlessly. Cheolsu said my pink sweater looked good on me. That was the only thing he said the entire way.

No one was home. His mother was at a relative's wedding and his little sister was still at school. In the living room an old carpet covered the floor and an unnaturally large television set clashed with an imitation Van Gogh hanging on the wall. Cheolsu made coffee and put on a record, some Jamaican artist I didn't recognize. Time was passing dully and I was getting antsy.

"Want to see my room?" Cheolsu finally asked.

I was dancing around to the thumping reggae music. Cheolsu had touched the coffee cup to his lips but didn't drink any. When he stopped the record, the grandfather clock on the wall suddenly rang out: *deng, deng, deng, deng*. The pale, hazy afternoon sunlight seeped through the window, and the dust rising off the carpet blurred my vision. The room was neither bright nor dark.

"My furlough ends the day after tomorrow," Cheolsu said as we went into his room.

Heavy winter drapes covered the window. A desk, a bookcase crammed with economics textbooks, a wardrobe, a bed, a pair of dumbbells: it was the same stuff you would find in any guy's room. In the low light I perused Cheolsu's books. I didn't recognize any of the titles. He didn't have any of the usual paperbacks or light essay collections or even any porn magazines stashed just out of sight. A glass top and a thin layer of dust that had accumulated during his four months away in the army covered the desk.

I'd known Cheolsu since high school.

He was two years older than I was and what I can only describe as ordinary. When I was a senior in high school, I worked part-time as a clerk at the local government office. Cheolsu was a college student and had come to the office on an errand. He earned some of the highest grades in his class and so it wouldn't be a stretch to say that he was a model student. By the time I finished college we weren't just friends, but we weren't exactly going steady either. What makes a relationship special? You talk on the phone every night before bed, hang out together every weekend, see new movies, remember each other's birthdays, and, assuming there are no particular problems, introduce one another to your parents at your graduation ceremonies. You think of each other when you're having a drink or watching porn, and gradually you come to understand all of life's standards through each other. When you define it that way, then Cheolsu and I were not special. He didn't make me feel anything, and I didn't make him feel anything. But oddly enough Cheolsu's friends and my friends all thought of us as a couple. Even my brother and sister thought so. *They'll get married someday*, they all thought. Neither Cheolsu nor I had ever talked about that, nor did we feel any particular need to. But perhaps after more time had passed and Cheolsu had matured and grown older and sprouted a few white hairs and wearied of time, and I too had wrinkled lips and ruined looks and had reached an age where there was no longer any trace of a flirtatious smile and no one would find me pretty, then maybe we truly would end up married.

"When my furlough is up, I'll report for duty at the Fifth Division in Yeoncheon. Two months there and then my military service is over."

"Seems like you're having an easy time."

"I know this doesn't carry much weight, but it *is* still the army."

"What will you do after you're discharged?"

"Guess I'll be unemployed at first."

I was standing in front of the bookcase and Cheolsu was by the closed drapes. His arms were resting awkwardly against the wall, as if unable to find the right spot. Time passed clumsily. Cheolsu came closer and put one arm around me. The silence was stifling. What came next? Neither of us knew. The whole time I'd known him this had never come up. How were you supposed to comfort a boy in the army?

"What do you want?" I asked, unable to bear the wait.

"To sleep with you."

"Why?"

"I dreamt about you."

"I don't have much time."

"It doesn't take that long."

"You've done it before?"

He just laughed and didn't say anything. Cheolsu's body looked drawn and hot, as if feverish—just being so near a girl's body seemed to excite him. So I pulled down my stockings and my panties, and after Cheolsu had touched me there for about three seconds, he said he couldn't wait any longer.

"Can I put it in?"

Cheolsu's room was silent and devoid of any draft; the air was as still as jelly. A drop of water falling in the bathroom sounded unnaturally loud. On instinct we tried to avoid making any noise. I nodded.

"But," I added, "you know you can't finish inside of me, right?"

"I know."

I wasn't at a risky point in my cycle or anything, but when boys are too selfish in their insistence, you always have to say that: *you can't have it entirely your way.*

It took him three tries to get inside me, and then he ejaculated too fast. It was probably over before he realized it. He didn't keep his promise to pull out. We got some tissue, cleaned up my soiled skirt and the floor, and got dressed. Just as he'd said, it didn't take that long. Then we sat apart from each other, looking in opposite directions.

That was what he'd wanted so badly? Boys were so strange.

Up until then he and I had never even held hands at the movies. So at that moment, touching Cheolsu's body was unfamiliar and uncomfortable.

"Cheolsu, did you turn off the record player?" I asked.

I thought I'd heard a faint sound coming from the living room a moment ago. During the very brief time that Cheolsu was inside me, I had sensed behind my back the bedroom door cracking open slightly and then closing again immediately. I was certain someone was in the living room, but I didn't mention it to him. He stood up, as if rescued from the moment by having something else to do, and said he wasn't really sure. When we went out to the living room, Cheolsu's mother was clearing away our coffee cups. Caught off guard, Cheolsu turned bright red. The zipper of his pants was still partway down.

"Mom, I thought you weren't coming home until later."

"I wasn't planning to but the wedding ended right away and there weren't that many people there. Who's this? A friend?"

I was certain that his mother had spied on us in his room, but she looked me right in the face and feigned ignorance. She didn't look anything like him. I never would have guessed that she was his mother. She was overweight and had a double chin, and her hair was as dry and curly as steel wool. Her face was shiny, like she'd just smeared on night cream. Her lips, painted brick red, were thick and crude, and the corners were drawn down wryly as she struggled to suppress her curiosity. There was nothing about her that brought to mind Cheolsu's pale skin and cool demeanor. But she smiled at me.

"Silly me, you must be his girlfriend! Is that why you two didn't hear me come in?"

"We were looking at my books," Cheolsu said dumbly.

His mother offered me some fruit. I told her I had to leave right away, but she insisted. I had no choice but to sit on the sofa and eat slices of banana and apple, and cookies that had grown mushy with age. Cheolsu was silent, and his mother studied me from head to toe with a sharp look in her eyes.

"Are you the same age as Cheolsu?"

"She's two years younger."

When Cheolsu answered for me, his mother glared at him.

"Was I asking you?"

Then she asked me a string of questions. What college had I gone to? Where did my parents live? How many siblings did I have? What did I major in? How was my health? Did I have a driver's license? A teaching license? Where did I work? How much money did I make? And so on, and so on. Far past the point of politeness.

"Mom, you just met her," Cheolsu said. "You can't grill her like that."

His mother ignored him and continued to ask me questions.

"What does your older brother do? You said there's a big age difference between you two?"

"He's preparing for a job in Japan."

I thought, to hell with it, and answered the question truthfully. I had already missed my chance to get to work on time.

"Oh, really? Fancy that. He must work with computers. Or something to do with art."

"No, he's applying for a job at a janitorial company."

"Janitorial?"

Her face changed color slightly, and she closed her mouth.

"Well, I'd better get going," I said. "I have to go to work."

"So soon? I hope you're not leaving on my account. It's okay—you should stay. Don't mind me."

"Mom, she said she has to go. She was supposed to leave by seven."

"When did I say she couldn't? So what does your father do for a living?"

As she walked me to the front door, she finally asked the question she'd wanted to ask in the first place, the one that had been driving her crazy with curiosity. Cheolsu's face turned red.

"He works for the government." He was on the verge of shouting. "The government! Are you also going to ask where *he* went to college and how much he makes and what he drives and what brand of tennis shoes he wears?"

Aghast, Cheolsu's mother looked at him as if to say, *Who would ask such an uncivilized question?* It was true that my father had once worked at city hall. But not anymore. Cheolsu didn't add that part, though. As soon as we got out of the house, he and I ran like mad for the bus stop. Luckily, the bus I had to take was just about to pull away. Cheolsu waved his arms wildly, while I ran until sweat broke out on my forehead. By the time I managed to clamber aboard the bus, I was too out of breath to even say good-bye.

Cheolsu waved and yelled, "Come see me next month on base?"

I nodded.

If you gently stroke my lips and the palm of my hand right now, you will find them strangely cold and icy, a feeling of endless distance that even I can sense. Someone once said to me, "You're so cold that I shake with despair. The whole time we're together your lips never once flush, and your body is like slippery ice. You have the eyes of a wolf-girl whose heart has never once been moved. When I press my ear to your chest, I hear only wind and emptiness."

Rain falls inside the dark, abandoned house. It streams down the walls of the kitchen and front door like a waterfall. Burn me. Pour gasoline over me and set my body on fire. Burn me at the stake like a witch. Wrap me in garbage bags and toss me in the incinerator. I'll turn into dioxin and make my way into your lungs. Stroke my face lightly with a razor blade and suck the blood that comes seeping out. Lap it up like a cat. I want to be covered in blood. I'll cry out in the end and weep for fear of leaving this world without ever once discovering the me inside me, the ugly something inside me. But then I see her: another me passing by like a landscape of inanimate objects outside the window of the empty house quietly collapsing in the rain.

Where have you been all this time? Were you off somewhere singing, putting cats to sleep on the porch, drifting about in the rapids of time, the glow of the morning sun and the rain of a summer afternoon beating down as you pass by, your lips shut tight like a bloodsucking plant? The me that is nowhere to be found now, the me that will turn to ash and vanish, turn to darkness and rot—that me extends a squalid hand at the final moment of this crash, having entirely deserted and abandoned my life. In truth, I was not me. The me that was born into an animal body and lived as a slave to poverty and insult was nothing but the emptiness that had been momentarily bewitched out of me by an evil spirit. That distant me is precious and beautiful. No matter how decadent and corrupt my body becomes, I will, like a desert orchid that blooms once every hundred years, come to you bearing this frigidness toward life.

I tell him, "All you have is my emptiness."

"Then where are you? The you that bleeds when I devour you like this?"

"You don't see? I just passed by outside that window and now I'm gone. This is the first and last time I will encounter you in this life. Give me some water. Sweat pours off of me like rain. You'll forget about me for the next hundred years. But leave your voice behind; when I come back to this place a hundred years from now, the moment I open the door a colony of bats and your voice will greet me."

"I'm taking my voice with me to the grave. I wouldn't leave it in a place like this. My blood is no vagrant."

"Then I'll become a snake and I'll find your grave."

"You're too lowly. You can't trespass upon a royal tomb."

The rain falls, lays siege to the world, as if it has been falling that way for years. The rain will fall even after the death of time. Roof half falling down. Windows broken. Kitchen dripping rainwater. Porch covered in filth. Creaky stairs covered in cats' paw prints. Dead rag doll, straw insides poking out. And, above all the gruesome things, our frigid relationship.

I couldn't believe it when Cheolsu's mother contacted me. I was working in the office at the university when she called.

"Who did you say is calling?"

"This is Cheolsu's mother."

I could practically see her stretching out the folds of her fat neck to make her voice sound more refined.

"Ah, yes. How are you?"

"You left so quickly the other night. You didn't even stay for dinner."

"I had to get to work."

"You were in such a hurry that I didn't have a chance to ask: What kind of work do you do? Cheolsu isn't very sociable. He never tells me anything. He's on leave from the army, but all he does is stay out late every night. Sons aren't sweet to their mothers. Not like daughters are."

"It's just a part-time job."

"Tutoring?"

"Nothing like that."

"Then what?"

I sighed, worn down by her stubborn refusal to give up.

"I wait tables."

"Oh my."

She was quiet for a moment, then started talking again before I could even begin to think about how to end the call.

"But you said you're a college graduate. You should be tutoring kids instead. That would be better for you. Cheolsu's little sister is still in college, but she's tutoring a high school student in math. She's good at math. She was planning to work only over vacation and then quit, but her student's mother begged her to stay. She said she's never seen a more talented tutor than my daughter. The father is a chief prosecuting attorney, but their kids aren't doing well in school. It worries them. Their father was a younger classmate of Cheolsu's father when they were in college, so that's how we know their family. And the job seemed reliable."

"Ma'am."

She was getting chattier by the minute, and I couldn't bear to hear another word. I decided I had to end the phone call, even if it meant being rude. It could also be that I was too angry to take any more.

"Ma'am, I'm busy right now. I have to hang up."

"My goodness, where is my mind?" she said, pretending to be apologetic. "Cheolsu said you're planning to visit him?"

"That's right."

"Are you going this weekend?"

"I haven't picked an exact date yet."

"Oh, no, I was certain Cheolsu said you're visiting him this weekend. I wanted to send him some food."

"They don't feed him in the army?"

I probably sounded curt. The more brusque my voice grew, the more slippery hers became, as if she were greasing her vocal cords.

"Of course they do, but you know it can't compare to food made by your own mother. It must be so hard for him there in training."

"He only has to serve for six months."

If she had suggested visiting him together, I absolutely would have refused. Promise or no promise, seeing Cheolsu was not worth putting up with that much indignity and discomfort.

"If you visit him this weekend, could you stop by our house first? I made chicken. It's not much; I promise it won't be too heavy. You two can eat it together when you see him. That'll be nice."

"You're asking me to take chicken to your son?"

To see Cheolsu, I would have to go all the way past the city of Uijeongbu, which I'd never been to before, transfer buses several times, go to a place called Yeoncheon, which I'd never even heard of, and find my way to an army base with a strange address. To top it all off, now I had to tote along a bundle of cold chicken like some kind of refugee. This was too much.

"I wish I could visit him myself." She sounded crestfallen. "But Cheolsu told me not to come. He said the other boys all have their girlfriends visit them and he'll be embarrassed if his mother shows up."

"Is that so?"

"I just want to feed my son his favorite dish, so though I know it's a burden for you, please do me this one favor. Anyway, he absolutely insists that I don't go, for fear of making his girlfriend uncomfortable."

She laughed. I pictured her eyes shining like a rat's when she peeped at us in Cheolsu's bedroom. I didn't want to have to look at her face again, but I figured one last time couldn't hurt. Once it was done, I would never have to see her again. So I gave in.

The last criminal sociology lecture was that Saturday night, but I requested the whole day off so that I could go see Cheolsu instead. In the end, I never got the chance to attend any of the lectures. Maybe if I had, it would have turned into a date. I pictured the instructor standing at the far end of the room, there, at the podium, while I sat in the very back in the dark, chewing on a pencil and listening to him talk about domestic violence. He would have been too far away to make out his face.

We all have many commonly held misconceptions about domestic violence. A typical example is the belief that domestic violence recurs in lower-class families or those with lower levels of education. Other examples include the assumption that the happier a family appears on the surface, the less likely they are to experience domestic violence; that when a child is abused, the abuser is whichever parent is less close to the child; that domestic violence within families is always linked to other social issues, such as broken homes, alcoholism, criminal records, and so on. These case studies show us that, just as with other social institutions, domestic violence has less to do with any inherent characteristics of the family as a primitive community of relatives and more to do with the changes wrought by modernization with its complex and diverse variables. As the causal factors, triggers, and control factors correlated with domestic violence intensify and diversify, it becomes harder for us to draw a clear conclusion.

The lecture would have gone on for three straight hours and ended with everyone turning in the homework. Since I wasn't a student, I would have torn out a piece of notebook paper and written this note for the instructor instead:

I sat in on your lecture today. I kept telling you I was too busy to go, so you probably didn't know I was there. To be honest, it was hard to follow. I've never taken any sociology classes or anything else like it, so of course it was new to me. I must confess that I was never a good student. You said you think you saw me last autumn when the fall semester was starting; that must have been at the tea party we held in the office to kick off the new semester. Since I don't know what any of the part-time lecturers look like, I don't remember meeting you. I've worked here for less than a year. I'll probably change jobs soon. I'm not a full-time employee—just a temp on a one-year contract. I don't know if you're teaching criminal sociology again next semester, but I don't think I'll be running into you at school anymore. Finals are next week, and then it's vacation. Winter is already here. Every time winter rolls around I find myself longing for things. A warm home. A heavy blanket. A wool sweater. A soft, light winter coat (that I can't afford). A kind word when times are tough. White snow falling on this dirty city. Stepping into a phone booth set in the middle of a street like a stage prop. A secret phone number in my hand that I can call at that very moment. The snowy night so quiet it seems to be holding its breath. Listening to "Stairway to Heaven" on repeat while waiting for a bus that never comes because the snow is falling too heavily and the traffic has come to a standstill.

It feels strange to have attended your last lecture and to write what will be my last and only letter to you. At any rate, you and I have never knowingly met. And though we might one day a long time from now cross each other's paths on the subway or at someone's funeral or at a highway rest stop, we won't recognize each other. It could indeed happen. For all we know we might even hold hands one day at a demonstration.

I'm not a member of any pacifist groups that denounce any and all antipersonnel weapons designed to hurt and kill people (and I don't believe you are either), but if I were to receive an invitation to one of their demonstrations, I would most likely cancel any unimportant plans I had in order to go (and I believe you would too). The people who go to those things cancel any unimportant plans they might have in order to attend, either alone or with family. There would be so many people that you and I could rub shoulders without realizing it. Everyone would clasp hands and form a human chain from one end of the city to the other. Human beings are capable of becoming perfectly pure at some moment in their lives. It doesn't matter if they're royalty or literati, middle class, working class, or the lowest class. For many people that moment must be the moment when they are clasping hands with each other. Memory finds its way back through blood, through body heat. Right at that moment.

But now is not that moment. Right now doesn't mean anything at all.

When I got home from work, I opened the kitchen cupboard to take out a loaf of bread and found a bottle of alcohol. My mother had started drinking again. I thought about getting mad at her but gave up on the idea. I must have been too tired. Getting drunk was her choice, as were her boozy-breath drunken ramblings that I hated listening to. Since her benders weren't that frequent, I could put up with this one for a little while. My mother didn't seem to care at all how badly she stank, or how ugly the whites of her eyes were, yellowed from the havoc she'd wreaked on her liver. She probably didn't remember anymore, but a long time ago, she'd won a Miss Cambison Ointment pageant. She'd stood onstage in the kind of bathing suit you might see on female divers and fluttered the false eyelashes she'd glued to her eyes. But now, it was comical to associate that memory with the mother who was standing in the kitchen, giving me the side-eye, with red marks on her cheek from the pillow and wearing ragged, dirty pajamas.

"What're you looking at?" she asked.

Tired of her gaze, I made toast and ranted inwardly: *You've been home all day. The least you could have done was make dinner. My brother thinks the kitchen is no place for men, and my little sister is probably eating instant noodles with her friends at school. When my brother saw there was no dinner, I bet he crinkled his face into a smile and went hungry without complaint.*

"No dinner. My brother must be starving," I said.

"I had to go back to work at the hospital because of him."

She forced her lipsticked mouth, which looked crumpled and crushed into a smile. She'd worked as a nurse before she started drinking. It was dirty work, too awful to describe. She did the kind of work that not even the patients' own flesh and blood would do for them. My brother had always felt guilty about the fact that she had to do such work, and when she lost her job because of her drinking, he said it was better that way.

"What happened?"

"He needs more money for Japan. I don't know why it's so complicated. I went to the hospital to see if they had any work for me."

"As if they'd have work for someone who drinks as much as you do."

"I don't drink. I told you I quit. I'm not lying." She shifted her eyes around nervously as she protested. "They said they're short on people lately and that I could start tomorrow. But even with an advance it won't be enough."

"How much more does he need?"

"A million *won*." She let out a sigh.

"What he's made so far doesn't cover it?"

"What do you expect? He didn't go to college, he has no skills, and his father and I are no help. Of course, he has no money to start a business of his own. He has an opportunity to earn money in Japan, but he doesn't have enough to get there, and there's no one he can borrow from."

"Do you ever worry about me or Mia as much as you worry about him?"

"You got to go to college," she said angrily. "Don't act all high and mighty just because you give me a little money to live on. You can barely make ends meet with that tiny paycheck of yours. The kids you went to school with are all working in banks and investment firms. They're making good money. But you make less than half of what they make, and still you complain all the time about how tired you are, and you make us all walk on eggshells around you. You owe me! Do you know how expensive it is to raise kids? Don't even think about leaving this house before you've paid it all back to me. You've got a long way to go."

The woman who called herself my mother opened her mouth wide and the reek of alcohol floated out, as usual. I put down my half-eaten toast and went into my room. For a moment, I considered whether they could rent my room out and make a little money that way. But the house was so old and dirty that there was no

way they would ever find a tenant. My mother continued to yell at me from the kitchen.

"I didn't think I'd be stuck living this way either!
You think you're so different from me? There's no
avoiding it—not once you're old and broke. You'll turn
out the same way. You better remember me as I am
now, because you'll turn out exactly the same. Nothing
will ever change!"

After my mother's voice faded, I heard the kitchen
cabinet open and the sound of alcohol pouring into
a glass. She gulped it down. After a few minutes of
silence, I heard sobs coming from Mia's room. My little
sister was crying.

The next morning I got up early and headed for
Cheolsu's house. The sky was overcast and the forecast
said the weather would be even worse by the afternoon.
It was as cold as it was hazy, and the damp, frigid air
seeped all the way down to my bones. My sister and
I had only one winter coat between the two of us. She
was younger and frailer than I was, so on winter mornings I usually told her to go ahead and wear it since I
wasn't that cold. That morning, as well, I left the house
with only my pink sweater for warmth. Cheolsu's

mother handed me the chicken in a disposable alumi-num container tucked inside a paper bag. The chicken was warm, but it would soon cool and turn hard as a rock. I couldn't stop myself from frowning. Cheolsu's whole family was sitting around the kitchen table. I turned down their offers of breakfast and told them I'd already eaten. His father said grace. The praying fam-ily looked pious and cultured. When I thought about the fact that Cheolsu had had these kinds of mornings the whole time he'd known me, my body twisted with awkwardness.

"This is Cheolsu's girlfriend. She's on her way to visit him today."

They all stopped eating and stared hard at me.

"Girlfriend? He never said anything about a girl-friend," Cheolsu's younger sister said, staring openly at my old, pilly sweater. "You know he tells me *everything*."

"Why would he tell you about his love life?" their mother said sternly. "Anyway, this is your brother's girl-friend, so be nice."

The family probably went on talking about me after I left. Cheolsu's sister would have said, "Why are her clothes so out of style? What school did she say she went to?" Cheolsu's father would have asked, "What does her father do? Do they go to church? Where did she graduate from?" Cheolsu's mother would have solemnly lectured her daughter that dressing neatly is all that matters, and she would've said that belittling someone for wearing old clothes is not the mark of a true human being. Then, when the daughter wasn't around, she would have told her husband what Cheolsu and I were doing when no one else was home. "We need to give him a good talking to, but we have to remain objective and not get emotional when we do. He's already an adult. He has to manage his own life. Could you talk to him? In the meantime, I'll keep pretending I didn't see anything." Cheolsu's father would momentarily experience the classic worry that *that girl* would be a ball and chain, an obstacle to Cheolsu's future.

It was a long way to the army base. I took a bus to the subway, then the subway to Uijeongbu, and then an intercity bus for miles and miles. The streets of Uijeongbu, where winter was just taking hold, were dull and deserted. The cold had come on quickly and frozen the streets lined with lonely restaurants and shady-looking bars. Near the army base lurked women in blue eye shadow and tight clothes that clung oddly to their bodies. A restaurant with faded roof tiles, called The Rose Garden, stood bleakly at the end of the road. A perfectly gray street. An old and dirty street. The Rose Garden didn't look anything like a rose. I sat on the intercity bus with no coat, as frozen as a scarecrow in an unsown rice paddy in the middle of winter, until the bus reached the stop where an old woman with chipped and worn nail polish told me I should get off. By the time I stepped off the bus in front of the army base in the middle of an empty field, Cheolsu's chicken in its paper bag was completely cold. The bus left. At least I was not the only woman there—it was the weekend, after all.

"Who are you here to see?"

Women—all there to visit soldiers—filled the PX. A guard wrote down my name and ID number with a black ballpoint pen.

"Kim Cheolsu."

The guard looked up at me. "Kim Cheolsu isn't here today. He's out on a training exercise."

"That can't be. He told me to come today."

"The exercise was announced at the last minute. But he's not far. I can tell you where to find him. Do you want to go visit him in the field?"

"Sure."

"It's about four kilometers from here. The bus will get you there right away, or you can walk. Just take any bus that stops out front, then get off in front of the fishing hole. There are signs pointing the way to the base HQ. Follow those signs and they'll lead you right to the drill field. It's easy. Just head there and you'll find him."

Soldiers who'd been called to the PX were checking in before meeting with their girlfriends, mothers, and younger sisters. I would rather have died than leave the warm PX and go back out into the cold, windy streets, but I had no choice. I picked up the bag of chicken and headed to the bus stop. I stamped my numb feet while waiting for the bus. Luckily, it didn't take long. I sat near the front. I was supposed to get off at a fishing hole? I tried to remember what the guard had said. *In front of the fishing hole.* The scenery outside the bus window looked completely different than before. Paddies and fields (I never could tell the difference between the two) and sheds and vacant houses whirled past. I couldn't tell anything apart, as though I was looking at a piece of film that kept replaying the same scene. A little kid in dirty clothes was sitting in the street in front of a house, crying with his mouth wide open. After the bus had taken several turns and gone over a hill, I saw the same little boy in front of the same house, still crying. Was it really the same kid? I looked around and tried to jog my memory. Identical vacant houses, fields, paddies, sheds, and bus stops slid past. How long had I been on the bus? It could have been hours, and it could have been only five minutes. Was this bus going in circles through the same village? The sky was as overcast as it had been early that morning, and it hung down dark and heavy, as if snow would come spilling down any minute. Then there was the static electricity of this ominous winter coldly dominating the whole world. I waited and waited, but the announcement for the bus stop in front of the fishing hole never came.

"Excuse me. I need to get off at the fishing hole. Is it still far away?" I asked the driver.

"Fishing hole? This bus doesn't go there," the driver said.

"Then where should I get off?"

"You'll have to get off at the next stop, cross the street, and catch another bus. It's quite far."

I knew the guard had said I could take any bus, but what could I do? I got off, sat on the bench at the desolate, abandoned bus stop, and waited for the next bus. I already regretted making this visit. A dog the size of a calf walked past me, carrying a dark red lump of flesh in its mouth. A dead rat, perhaps. Snow began to fall. It settled into a thin layer on my hair and my old sweater. The dog with the rat in its mouth turned to me with empty eyes, huffing and panting. I thought that maybe it was studying the bag of chicken in my hand. It looked like it had something to say to me.

Give me some chicken and I won't eat you.

A bulletin board beside the bus stop displayed a "Wanted" flier. There were none of the usual movie posters or nightclub ads. I read the flier out loud to try to stave off the cold.

Wanted by police: One female, last seen with dyed hair and wearing baggy pants; and two males, both wearing basketball sneakers. Suspects are believed to be drifters from the city. On September 4, Kim (alias), a thirty-nine-year-old male resident of Seoul, and Jeong (alias), a twenty-seven-year-old female resident of Uijeongbu, were found murdered. Reports indicate that Kim was escorting Jeong home after they had dinner together at The Rose Garden. Kim was killed by repeated blunt force trauma to the back of the head, and his body was found on the side of the road leading up to Jaein Waterfall in Yeoncheon. Time of death is estimated at 8:00 a.m. on September 4. Around 9:00 a.m. of the same day, Yi Sun-im, Jeong's sixty-year-old landlady, heard groans coming from Jeong's room and found her with multiple stab wounds to the head and chest. Jeong was transferred to the hospital but passed away at 2:00 p.m. The car that Kim and Jeong left The Rose Garden in has yet to be found. According to anonymous witnesses, after eating dinner Kim stated that he would drive Jeong home, and they left the restaurant together. In the parking lot, some unidentified youngsters who appeared to be hippies from the city tried to hitch a ride and became angry when Kim refused them. Witnesses say they cursed at him and then disappeared into the dark. Police found no leads to suggest that anyone had a grudge against Kim, or that he had been in any financial disputes, and there were no indications that he was involved in any

sexual affairs. Therefore the police are investigating this group of youngsters as the prime suspects in this case. The suspects are believed to be in their early to midtwenties. They are described as vulgar of speech and poorly dressed, and the woman's hair is dyed wine red. They've been spotted frequently in red light districts and up in the hills near Daegwang-ri, Uijeongbu, and other nearby cities. Kim was driving a black Sable. Anyone with any information on these suspects or who may have spotted these individuals is asked to contact the Yeoncheon Police Department.

The whole time I was reading the flier the dog kept pacing around the bus stop. September 4. That means the crime had happened over three months ago. Had their murder become this village's great unsolved mystery? Or was it simply that nothing else had happened after the case was solved, so they forgot to take down the flier? Just as I was debating whether to give the chicken to the dog, the bus came.

When I got off at the fishing hole, there were signs pointing the way to the base. The signs directed me to a steep, narrow mountain path. The snow was still falling and the path was dark. I popped into a store near the bus stop and asked for a cup of instant coffee to warm myself up. I felt feverish. My shoulders and hair were damp. Once I felt a little warmer, I started walking up the path to the base. Under my jeans, my legs had long since lost all feeling. I stopped thinking about why I had come all that way, what Cheolsu was to me, and whether I had a future. How long had I been out in the cold? I was hungry and dizzy. I was freezing but craved a glass of cold water at the same time. I sat on the side of the road and absentmindedly reached into the bag of chicken. I thought I would have just a bite, but when I opened the aluminum container and saw the chicken carcass looking like the body of a woman frozen to death in Siberia, I lost my appetite. Fortunately the snow wasn't sticking; it was settling lightly on the ground and melting away like dew. Had it not melted, I would have wished for the snow to turn sharp instead. Turn sharp and pierce through me. I arrived at the base entrance and told the guard I was there to see Officer Kim Cheolsu, who was on a training exercise.

"Ah, you mean Officer-in-Training Kim Cheolsu?" The guard was friendly. "If you head up that way, you'll see a burned clearing. That's where everyone should be."

"Is it far?"

"No, it's not far. You just can't see it from here because of the tree cover."

A burned clearing: that was how the guard had described it. And just as he said, in the middle of the forest I came across a deep water hole that appeared from between blackened and burnt trees, a huddle of soldiers, and fire. The soldiers had gathered firewood and were clustered around a bonfire. Dark, shining faces that I couldn't tell apart. Cheolsu's face was not among them. But then again Cheolsu's face could have been planted right before my eyes and I would have walked on past, too full of disappointment to recognize him. The soldiers' faces were that uniform, and that unfamiliar. I told them I was looking for Kim Cheolsu. They looked around at each other and shook their heads. The paper bag with Cheolsu's chicken fell from my hand. Out past the treeless clearing I saw a white cliff wall, and somewhere a crow let out a sharp cry. The wind blew through the branches and scattered the lacework of snow that had settled there. The wind flattened the tall autumn grass that had not yet died.

"I came all this way because I was told he was here."

There were about ten soldiers gathered around the fire. None of them spoke, as if the wind had frozen their mouths shut. Their lips looked chapped and malnourished. I stared at the cliff wall.

Cheolsu, where are you?

After a dull and interminable length of time had passed, one of them finally spoke.

"Kim Cheolsu didn't come to training."

"But I was told he was here."

They kept quiet. Branches crackled and snapped in the fire. I bent over to pick up the bag of chicken.

"We have some hot water. Would you like some?"

I accepted a cup of the water that had been boiling in a camping pot. A stab of pain ran through my head like a knife. I felt frozen. I sat down on the snow-dampened mud with the soldiers.

"Kim Cheolsu didn't report for training," the soldier repeated.

"But they told me he did."

"There must have been a mistake. Maybe they confused him with the Kim Cheolsu who was in an accident."

"What do you mean, 'the Kim Cheolsu who was in an accident'?"

The hot water exploded in my head. The soldiers stopped talking again, as if they didn't know what they should say. None of them appeared to be in charge. That's probably why they weren't sure how much they should tell me.

"Actually, there are two officers-in-training named Kim Cheolsu," said the soldier.

I didn't respond.

"The Kim Cheolsu who was supposed to be on this training exercise isn't here. I'm not sure which one you're looking for, but you should go back to the base where you first checked in. The Kim Cheolsu who is there is probably the one you're looking for."

There were two officers-in-training here with the same name. No one had told me, and I never would have guessed. Maybe one of them really was the Kim Cheolsu I knew. All I did know was that, for reasons unknown to me, I could not meet the Kim Cheolsu

66

who had been here. I would never get to see the Kim Cheolsu who'd met with some mysterious accident on a snowy winter day. If I went back to the beginning, there would be another Kim Cheolsu, and I would be able to find him. No one knew if that Kim Cheolsu was the one I knew, the one I'd wandered all that way for, carrying a bag of chicken to give to him.

"I'll head back."

I handed back the hot water and nodded good-bye to the soldier who'd spoken to me.

"Wouldn't you like to warm up a little before you go?"

He looked at me with sympathy. I wanted to stay there forever. Give Cheolsu's chicken to a rabid dog to rip apart and eat. But instead I stood and watched the crows as they dove from the cliff. I couldn't bring myself to approach the blazing fire. Where was Cheolsu? Was he here? Was he there? Had the Cheolsu I was looking for died in some accident? Was he in the hospital? Or was he sitting with the other middle-class officers-in-training, surrounded by giggling girlfriends and mothers and sisters, laughing and joking over shots of alcohol, having forgotten all about me and the stupid chicken? What was real and what was fantasy? And what was it that I really wanted—reality or fantasy? The same old apathetic Cheolsu who'd been waiting a long time for his chicken, or the malnourished Cheolsu out here with the crows at the bottom of that cold cliff?

When I returned to the first base, other soldiers were signing in for visits at the PX. Just as I had before, I gave my name, ID number, and address and said I was there to see Kim Cheolsu. The soldier pointed to where he was sitting. He was on a bench beneath a tarp roof. He was with the other officers-in-training and their girlfriends, mothers, and sisters who'd come to visit them, drinking cheap whiskey—alcohol that was officially forbidden on base. They were giggling, and everything was exactly as I had imagined it. I walked over to Cheolsu, whose back was turned to me, but still I could see he was laughing. Someone nudged him in the side and whispered something in his ear. Finally he noticed me. The closer I got, the more people turned to stare. They stopped laughing. The girlfriends and mothers and little sisters stopped smiling and looked at me warily. The snow was still falling, but they didn't look cold in their wool coats.

"What took you so long?" Cheolsu asked awkwardly, taking the tattered paper bag of chicken from my clenched hand. "I couldn't wait any longer and decided to join my friends. We've been talking about how to build bridges. One of the guys specializes in bridge construction."

Bridge construction. Building bridges. I didn't hide the look of scorn on my face. Cheolsu was probably hurt, but he didn't say anything in front of his friends.

"Would you like a cookie?"

One of the girlfriends offered a plate of cookies and sliced fruit. The faces and clothing of the women gathered on the bench in the falling snow were so different from my own. Their breath came out white. I shook my head coldly, without saying a word. Cheolsu took my hand and wrapped his arm around my shoulders.

"Let's go over there to talk."

Get your hands off me. Don't stroke my face. I'm not an animal.

Why was I suddenly thinking that?

I felt doubtful, but Cheolsu looked straight ahead as we walked.

"I wrote to my mom. Told her not to come. I told her it would make you too uncomfortable."

"It didn't matter to me."

"But it did." He sounded upset. "You took so long that I thought you weren't coming."

"I left early this morning."

"Then what happened? It's almost three p.m."

"The guards at the PX told me you were doing a training exercise at a different base. I went all the way to the other base, on the other side of a snow-covered mountain, but they told me you were here. They said there are two officers-in-training named Kim Cheolsu. The other wasn't there because he got in an accident during training, so they sent me back here. They said you were probably the Kim Cheolsu I was looking for. I came all the way back, worried I might never see you again."

The words came out so fast that I wasn't sure I even believed myself. I stopped. No further explanation seemed necessary. Cheolsu probably felt the same. He listened to me with his mouth half-open and didn't say anything for nearly a minute.

"What are you talking about? You think there are like five hundred officers-in-training here? I'm the only Kim Cheolsu. There's been a huge misunderstanding. If you don't believe me, go ahead and ask someone else."

I didn't understand what was going on either. Was this hatred I was feeling? Or a dull affection buried deep inside? Or was I merely acting out some dramatic emotion in order to endure this chaotic life? I had no idea. *But for God's sake, stop petting my shoulder like that. I'm not an animal.*

After a brief silence he asked, "Did you eat?"

We held hands as we walked. Like two lovers on a snowy, unpaved road. I shook my head.

"There's not much to eat here. Just cookies." Cheolsu sounded apologetic, and then he held up the bag of chicken as if he'd suddenly remembered it was there. "We have this!"

I shuddered in horror.

"I hate chicken. Besides, that's for you."

"Says who?"

"I have to go to the bathroom."

"It's over there."

Cheolsu pointed to the soldiers' latrines at the end of the parade ground. I went inside and squatted down awkwardly, trying to keep my body from touching the latrine door, and peed for a long time. My thighs and bottom were ice cold. When I came out, Cheolsu was pouring a can of Coke into two paper cups. He was sitting on a bench beneath a tree overlooking the snowy parade ground. Cheolsu's friends and their girlfriends, mothers, and little sisters were staring at us from across the way. They looked like they were waiting to see how much I would enjoy eating his chicken.

"Here, dig in."

He tried to hand me some Coke. I shook my head.

"Eat! I bet you haven't eaten anything all day," he said, tearing up the chicken.

"Cheolsu, are there two Kim Cheolsus here?"

"Huh?"

He put down the chicken and looked at me.

"Tell me. Is there another officer-in-training named Kim Cheolsu besides you?"

"I told you there isn't. Someone made a mistake. Either you misheard them or some idiot private misunderstood you. Besides, what does it matter? You're here now, and the Kim Cheolsu you were looking for is right in front of you. So who cares? Have some chicken."

"It's *your* chicken." I pushed away his hand as he held out the carcass. "Cheolsu is a very common name. You know that."

"What the hell are you getting at?"

"I know I said your name clearly, both here and at the other base. Kim Cheolsu. I said I was here to meet Kim Cheolsu. Just like that. But the soldier at the drill field told me, 'The Kim Cheolsu who was supposed to be on this training exercise isn't here. I'm not sure which one you're looking for, but you should go back to the base where you first checked in. The Kim Cheolsu who's there is probably the one you're looking for.' That's what he said."

"You're tired." Cheolsu gazed into my eyes as if to soothe me. "That's why your nerves are frazzled. Have some chicken. You'll get your strength back, and you'll feel better. Do what I say."

My eyes started to well up with tears. Up until that moment I'd never really understood sadness. The fierce, mob-like sadness that would come over me, clear and strong. Where did it come from? Was it real? This sadness that crept up and cut through all of my routines and my boredom and my repetition and my drama, like a sliver of glass piercing my flesh and sticking in the soles of my feet?

"I went to see your mother," I said. "She called me."

I ignored Cheolsu's chicken and kept talking. He must have seen my tears, but he wouldn't move his hand away, which was still holding the carcass.

"I really don't belong with you. If it was like the old days, when all we did was bump into each other at the bus stop on the way home from school and say hello, that would be one thing, but this isn't it."

"What are you saying?"

"I hate the formulaic lives you and your mother lead."

Finally, I'd said it.

"Don't say that. Eat some chicken."

It seemed like Cheolsu was suppressing his anger, or his wounded pride. His voice was high and peevish. I took the chicken, placed it back in the container, and put it in the torn paper bag. Cheolsu watched wordlessly. I carried the bag over to the latrines. The snow was falling prettily on the paper bag that held the chicken carcass, on my footprints, on my sweater, and on the soldiers' latrines, like a drawing of a landscape at midnight. The weather was frighteningly dark, and the world was filled with shadows that made it impossible to tell the time. I tossed Cheolsu's chicken into the latrine and turned around. Cheolsu was standing right behind me. I ignored him and walked away. His friends, and their girlfriends, mothers, and little sisters were still staring at us.

"I'll never forgive you for this. Ever," Cheolsu hissed at me as I brushed past him. "All you do is put up walls and make excuses that I can't understand. I've always hated people who go through life as if they don't care, making everyone else pander to their moods. I tried to feel a sense of duty toward you."

Without looking at him, I said, "Now that your toilet has eaten your chicken, you've done your duty."

And then I left.

I became very ill after returning home. I had a fever and my body broke out in hives. My room was covered in dust from not having been cleaned in a long time, and at night I heard rats scuttling around. No one opened my door to check whether I was alive or dead. At work they were planning a Christmas party; they called to ask whether I could make it. One of the women who worked in the university office told me that it had been snowing the entire time I was sick, and there was a big commotion because everyone who'd taken a weekend trip to Gangwon Province was stuck there. On the third day, after my fever lifted, I took some bread and butter out of my desk drawer and ate it with barley tea. The cold butter and the lukewarm tea sat in my mouth. My brother's departure date for Japan was approaching. He told me he was going to take out a loan to cover the rest of the money he needed. He put on a black fur-lined hat, black boots, and black gloves. He looked like an aging thief.

"I'll send you money," he promised me. "Mia is starting high school next year, and you'll need money for your wedding. Stop working nights at that restaurant. I'll send you money."

"I'm never getting married."

"Of course you will. You'll marry Cheolsu," he said, grinning.

Don't say that, brother. You know as well as I do that this is all just theater.

I went with my brother to the bank so that he could take out the loan, and on the way back we had our photograph taken. I combed my hair neatly and reapplied my lipstick in the mirror at the photo studio. Our family had never taken a picture together in a studio. But there it was, right on the way home, as if we were seeing it for the first time. My brother stroked my hair and said, "Let's take a picture." We held hands in front of the camera. His hand was hot, as if he had a fever. Then both of our hands were sweating. If I never saw him again after that day, I would think of him a hundred years from now. That photo of him was the last I would see of his face. His final face in some distant future. My brother and I clasped hands tightly, sweat slicking our palms, as if we'd planned it that way from the start.

Then, just like that, he left for Japan with the other employees of the janitorial company. I did not attend the Christmas party at work. My mother and I made Christmas cards to send to people in prison. It was so cold in our poorly heated house that we had to keep blowing on our hands as we worked. When the new year began, I would have to find a new job. Each morning I opened my frost-covered window and looked down at the dead, bony trees lining the road. A new low-income apartment building was going up across the street. That meant the dye factory next to its polluted stream would shut down, but I did not yet hear the sound of construction.

"If only he could have worked at that construction site instead of going so far away," I muttered to myself.

My mother paused in the middle of gluing a card and shook her head.

"No, men are supposed to aim high and strike out on their own," she said, her voice filled with conviction. "They can't get by as day laborers forever."

"Do you really think he'll come back?"

I stared out the window as I asked. Maybe she did know everything after all. At least on days like today, when she wasn't drinking.

"Of course. That child came out of my belly. No one knows him better than I do. I have faith."

She was unshakable. She kept brushing on glue and did not turn to look at me. Perhaps I still had something to learn from her, my poor alcoholic mother. Despite having eaten at the same dinner table with my family long enough to feel ashamed of them and turn red with embarrassment because of them and feel wretched with them and never breathe a word of my own feelings to them, I would in the end encounter that other me in the mirror. Maybe with time Cheolsu and I would become similar people who sit at a similar table and have similar conversations over dinner and then appear in my mirror. The Cheolsu in the mirror hands me the frozen chicken carcass.

There. Have some chicken. You'll feel better.

Cheolsu, I will eat your chicken when that day comes. I will gladly become your toilet. When I can, for once in my life, for a brief moment, become ardently pure. When that day comes.

"Did you have a nice visit with Cheolsu?" my mother asked out of the blue.

"That was a while back."

"How is he?"

"I didn't see him."

"You didn't see him?"

"Nope. Cheolsu wasn't there."

Cheolsu was not there. Cheolsu fell like a crow from a white cliff while I wandered through a village of soldiers in the snow carrying Cheolsu's dead chicken before returning home and falling ill. Did Cheolsu know? Cheolsu grows up to become his mother and his father. Just as I grow up to become my mother and my father. But the other Cheolsu, who fell from the white cliff, and I would pass by in silence outside the window of an abandoned house in the rain. Rain falls on the corpses of time.

My mother and I put the finished Christmas cards and candy in envelopes.

"You and Cheolsu don't make sense together. I never understood why you two were so close for so long."

"You don't have to understand it. But he's gone now. I won't be seeing him again."

"He was stupid and slow."

"Please, I beg of you, stay out of it. What do you know anyway?"

Would my father get his card and his candy? Before he went to prison, he told us, "I want to kill myself. I didn't do anything wrong. Send me letters on poisoned paper. I'll swallow them whole."

Instead we sent him poison-free Christmas cards and candy. For all I knew, he might have eaten every page of every book we ever sent him. He'd have been better off looking for a different method. My little sister pranced into the room. Her latest dream was to become a model. Up until recently it'd been to become a beautician. She said she didn't remember much about our father.

"Studying sucks," she said, tossing her book bag on the floor before taking off her shoes. "I'm not going to study anymore. I don't know why anyone would throw their whole body and soul into something so pointless. Being first in class or getting perfect grades is easy as long as you set your mind to it, but I can't see myself doing only that all the time. There are so many other things that I could be doing."

She was the only one among us who had hopes for her future.

"I'm going to be a lesbian when I grow up," she told me, as I jotted down a note in the card for our father. "Then I'll be in a whole new world. There's got to be something completely different out there—not just what our eyes can see. My friends think it's a genius idea."

She was talking about transcending your origins and your own willpower. Since she was the only one among us who'd gone on a class trip, maybe she could actually accomplish the things she said. Each time I wrote a note to my father, I hesitated. I knew full well that what my father wanted was not these silly notes telling him how the family was doing. Silence. The silence inside a prison. The prison of time called life. The prison of class and circumstance. The prison of a code untranslatable into the language of the other. The prison of the flesh. The prison of sweaty hands that can't let go even at the moment of falling. The prison of Cheolsu.

Dear Father,

Our older brother has left for Japan. His visa is only good for one year, but he might never come back. He will spend the rest of his life in Osaka's sewer, inside tunnels flowing with black wastewater, because down there the police don't bother looking for illegal immigrants. Mother had only half a bottle of soju yesterday. She sobered up after an hour.

He wouldn't be interested in reading any of that. Mother was writing the same letter she wrote every year, a letter she would send to an advocacy group. An endless litany of excuses regarding an old incident that no one cared about or believed in anymore.

"It'll be different this time."

She never lost hope.

"The church has taken an interest in my letter. Eventually they too will believe me when I say that he didn't abuse his power to take bribes or make himself rich through illegal means. There might even be protests in front of the courthouse or the prison."

"Does this church know that you drink?"

"The church will help."

"Mother, he's not an activist or a political prisoner or even a prisoner of conscience. Don't you get it? These days, if you're not one of those people, then no one cares."

"But he is innocent!"

"What does it matter now? Besides, do you really believe that? I don't."

"What are you talking about?"

"The truth is that, one way or another, he was corrupt. I don't think anyone is really qualified to say they got a fate they didn't deserve. No one is ever completely innocent."

"You're calling your father corrupt? You throw around such dangerous words as if they're nothing! There was no proof, no witnesses. They used him."

"That's what they call mass hypnosis, Mother. Do you really think that analyzing everything from an antiestablishment perspective will give you the answer you want?"

"Then I suppose you think it's right that we have to live this way? Maybe you can accept it, but I can't. Everyone at city hall knows that your father was a scapegoat. They promised to look after us. They said they would take care of our living expenses. I haven't heard from anyone."

"Everyone, including you and me, is living the life they had coming to them. Don't you get it? It's not about corruption or crime or conscience."

"Of course you would say that. You were born with a knife in your heart. That's why I'm no longer surprised by anything that comes out of your mouth."

A demonstration had been taking place in front of the prison since dawn. Some political prisoners who'd violated the National Security Law were in the same prison as my father. I heard they'd started a hunger strike in response to the prison guards' unjustified use of excessive force. The prisoners' family members were demonstrating to try to pressure the prison into moving one of the men to a hospital, as he had swallowed a dozen nails while calling for retribution. I wrapped a scarf around my throat and walked along the wall of the prison. The final sun of that winter was nowhere in sight. The crowd of demonstrators was growing larger by the minute, and the prison doors remained closed. It would be hard to get inside for a visit today. I left when the television crews arrived. Where had the political prisoner found twelve nails? If you swallowed twelve nails, would they slowly kill you? A group of men who looked like university students got off a bus; they wore backpacks that clanked with Molotov cocktails. Two of them approached me.

"There's a rally tonight. We must all stand together."

"Come with us. The dawn of the people has not yet risen."

I passed by those hot-blooded partisans and bought a cup of instant coffee to sip as I walked to the bus stop. I waited awhile and then bought another cup. The shadows of the brave receded. I took out the card I was planning to send to my father and, while standing there on the windy street, jotted something down on the back of it.

Dad, swallow nails.

That was everything that happened in 1988.

That year was my beginning and my end. It was one year of my life that was neither particularly unhappy nor particularly happy. It wasn't so different from 1978, and it wasn't any more or less memorable in comparison to 1998. The things that happened in 1988 had also happened in 1978 and would happen again in 1998. The people I met in 1988 were no different from those who bumped shoulders with me in the subway in 1978 and whose apathetic eyes met mine outside of a gas station in the middle of the night in 1998. They were family, and they were the unfamiliar middle class, and they were malnourished soldiers. They were each other's toilets and strangers and cliffs and crows and prisons. They were never anything more than who they were. Third person random.

I went through a number of different jobs after 1988. The university offered to extend my contract for another year, but instead I worked at a law office that my father's friend had connected me with, because the pay was higher. I quit my part-time job at the restaurant. After the law office, I worked in the public relations office of a department store and at the in-house magazine of an automobile company. Now and then I got to take photographs of buildings, interview people, and write articles. The work wasn't so different from what I did in 1988, except that typewriters changed to word processors, which soon changed to personal computers. Late at night I would lean back in my office chair and listen to K. D. Lang's "Barefoot" thirteen times in a row. Exactly thirteen times. At ten o'clock, the lights shut off throughout the building and the flashing lights of cars all pointed in the same direction, like stars floating below the surface of a river. I would listen to the song on repeat with my legs propped up on the desk and my back pressed against the chair, and when it ended, I would spring up out of my chair like a corpse come back to life and pace back and forth across the darkened office.

And I talked to people here and there. At the bus stop, in the subway, at the office, or the park, or the police station, or the shop that sold ramen boiled in a large iron pot. Sometimes it was for work, and sometimes it was a wrong number, and sometimes it was a friend whose name I called out, and sometimes it was someone I wanted to get to know better. There were people I saw nearly every day, and there were business relationships, and there were people I wanted to have a drink with, and people who wanted to borrow money from me, and people I wanted a shot at seducing once we got to know each other better. And then sometimes there were strangers I'd never met before.

"I was in the Fifth Division in 1988."

That's how he began it.

"I see."

"I was doing my compulsory service."

I said nothing.

"I think I saw you."

I laughed. I laughed without making any sound so the person on the other end of the phone couldn't see me smiling. He probably took it as mere silence.

"It was a gray, snowy day," he said, not paying my silence any mind.

"You have no idea who I am, and yet you're telling me all of this."

"Indeed," he conceded. "We've never met, at least not that we were aware of."

"I don't know you."

"I was about to tell you who I am."

"I'll give you one minute. Starting now."

I didn't bother to look at the clock.

"In 1988 I served as an officer-in-training in the Fifth Division in Yeoncheon. Everyone thinks that rank was invented just to give the presidents' sons an easier time during their conscription, but luckily even some of us sons of poor families could benefit from it as long as we were able to pass the officer candidate test. Wow, that was already ten years ago. I teach sociology courses at a university, but I'm not a full professor. I'm what you might call an after-hours club performer—a part-time outside lecturer who teaches night classes. By day I'm an ordinary company employee. The official title of my course is criminal sociology; I lecture for three hours straight. The topic changes every week: murder, robbery, burglary, rape, domestic violence."

"What kinds of people commit murder?"

"Murderers, I suppose."

"Your minute is up."

"Do you suppose we will ever be rid of all antipersonnel weapons?"

"Huh?"

"How are such weapons any different from murder?"

"They're not."

"I'm planning a demonstration. Everyone will form a human chain."

"Doing that won't change a single thing."

"Will you join us anyway?"

"I might have plans."

"The people who come to these things are willing to cancel any unimportant plans in order to be there."

"You're a rare sort of idealist."

"I might be the complete opposite."

"I've changed a lot. You probably won't recognize me."

Oddly enough, time repeated itself. It outlived memory. Back then Cheolsu was nowhere to be found, and it would be no different in the future. Meaningless sensations lingered on my skin as clearly as teeth marks that refused to fade. Time pushes away that which is intended, rejects that which is rejected, forgets that which is sung about, and is filled with that which it turns its eyes from, such as the white hairs of a loved one.

After my brother left, after about a year had passed, we were no longer able to stay at number 16, where we'd been living. According to the district office, construction of the new apartment building had weakened the ground and put neighboring houses that had not been rebuilt in danger of collapsing. Our home was no more. Number 25. Number 337. Number 1115. All of the places where we lived. We lost touch with my brother—he never wrote, and he never sent money. I do not think of it as a betrayal. What my brother had promised when he squeezed my sweaty hand as if he'd never let go was not money or letters. It was the erasure of time that goes by the name of money and letters. I understood that. The sort of time in which people could become the purest they'd ever been; cancel any unimportant plans they had; and long for a random, distant ideal. Our blood, which refused to be moved by a warm prayer over breakfast, a conversation with a loving family, a life that evolves step by step—that was what made my brother free. My brother, who was somewhere in the dark sewer tunnels of Osaka. I loved that brother. Not because he was family or because he'd bought me a washing machine. What he had left to me was a long-long-lived frigidity. The stillness of a beautiful, taxidermied want.

"Don't you dare think of leaving."

My mother had a lot of worries about me.

"You're still a long way from paying me back. Your debt won't be over until I'm dead. Not ever."

My mother worried for no reason. She would outlive all of us. That was the truth. My bright, clever little sister never became a beautician or a model or a lesbian. That was sad. Sadness made her hair fall out.

When she'd lost nearly all of her hair, she spoke to me from inside the mirror.

"Sister, I'm turning into taxidermy."

I go in search of number 16. When I insert the key, the lock creaks with rust before finally opening. The rain falls hard. The house is a mess; the roof is close to caving in. The walls that haven't toppled over sit askew, as if the ground below them is slowly sinking. Nearly all of the walls drip with rainwater. Black spiders spin webs; the electric lights are broken. The windows are all shattered and no light comes in. It was once a four-room house with a kitchen and a bathroom, but now it stands in the shadow of twelve-*pyeong* apartments, its walls covered in blue mold. The smell: awful.

The man stands in the courtyard as if he does not dare step inside a house like this. No one would have ever actually lived in such a place. The first time he touches me, he says, "Tell me, who was the first man you slept with?"

"I can't remember."

"Don't lie," he says. "Tell me. It's okay."

"I told you I can't remember."

"How old did you say you were? Seventeen? Who was he? A local gang member? An older boy at your church? Your high school physics teacher? Or did you do it at a bar for money?"

In a flash his face twists with fear and desire and disillusion. I work hard to become his fear and desire and disillusion. It comes back simultaneously as my own fear and desire and disillusion. He enjoys seeing another version of himself through me, a version that he could never become.

"You're cold. Cold as winter rain. A woman like you deserves to be punished," he says. "Get down and crawl like a dog."

Just then I walk by outside the darkened window.

Static electricity raises goose bumps on my skin.

It is my first time encountering myself. I walk on by without looking. There is no smell, no trembling. I've heard that what appears in a hallucination is an image of the dead.

"What's wrong with you?" he asks.

"I just walked past the window."

"What?"

"I walked by. I see myself for the first time."

He lets out a small laugh and ignores me.

"This place is going to fall down at any second."

"It was diagnosed as falling a long time ago."

"It's a dump."

"This is where I was born and grew up."

"I never would've figured you for lower class."

"Where were you in 1988? Were you in Yeoncheon, by any chance?"

"Don't be stupid. I was in the United States."

"When you were in the United States, did you ever dream about snow falling on a military base near a fishing hole? About malnourished soldiers and a dead chicken?"

"Why would I see that in a dream?"

He picks up off a chair a photo that is soiled with dust and the carcasses of spiders and the footprints of mice. He flicks his lighter and takes a long look at it. It's the portrait of my brother and me taken at the photo studio when 1988 was ending. The last photo of us, where we held each other's sweaty hand and he clung desperately to mine as if crazed and swore that he would take care of me and that things would be easier from then on. The last photo from a hundred years later.

"Is this you?" he asks, pointing to me in the photo.

"Yes."

"Who's he?"

"My brother."

"He looks a lot older than you."

"Ten years."

"Where is he now?"

"Probably in the sewers of Osaka. He's been living there for a long time now."

"Strange family."

He moves the lighter away from the photo and over to my body. He holds it close to my face. The light dazzles my eyes and I blink. He's an especially visual creature. When the lighter hovers by my crotch, he asks, "Can I burn you a little?"

I nod and shut my eyes. Burn me. Pour gasoline over me and set my body on fire. Burn me at the stake like a witch. Wrap me in garbage bags and toss me in the incinerator. I'll turn into dioxin and make my way into your lungs. Stroke my face lightly with a razor blade and suck the blood that comes seeping out. Lap it up like a cat. I want to be covered in blood. I'll cry out in the end and weep for fear of leaving this world without ever once discovering the me inside me, the ugly something inside me. The foul scent of burning hair. The heat.

"I'll make you grind against my toes, and then I'll come on your face," he says.

And then he does.

He and I walk out into the waterfall of rain. Number 16 is empty again and left to the country of mold and spiders. On rainy nights like this, people linger in their houses, afraid to so much as breathe too loudly. He and I are hungry.

"Let's go get something to eat," he says.

"I hate chicken. Anything is fine as long as it's not chicken."

The rain flows along the streets, down, down to the low spots. In silence we pass the lonely deserted main drag, the neighborhood under redevelopment where the subway construction is not yet finished, the old apartment complex, the street with the run-down bars. From the vending machine at a closed gas station, we each get instant coffee and share a joint. The filter keeps us from getting too high, so we have no problem driving.

"I'm not that into this," I say.

"Then where should we go?" he asks.

"The Rose Garden."

"That's in Thailand."

"It's on the way to Yeoncheon."

"Yeoncheon is too far. You want to drive all the way to the border?"

"It's not as far as the border. We'll be there in no time."

"Long way to go for a bite to eat."

"There's nowhere else to eat at this hour."

Clouds drift through my head. Blue sky so deep you'd never know the end of it, clouds from Africa, a slow-moving breeze, thunder and lightning. Pacing in front of a gas station on a night as black as lacquer. An hour when even the radio is silenced by rain. I finally spot The Rose Garden. It is older and more run-down and out of place in this world. Bricks line the gray dirt courtyard devoid of even a single rosebush.

He parks the car in the lot and says, "What the hell is this? It's closed!"

The whole world has quieted down because of the rain. Figures of people appear and disappear in the darkness. One woman and two men. The woman is wearing large, baggy pants, and her hair is dyed wine red. The men are wearing basketball shoes. They look rough, like hoodlums. It is so dark out that I see them brushing past the car like ghosts, but he does not. I realize then that I have brought him to the center of my bleak hour. He leaves teeth marks on my arm that will outlast memory. I look at his white hairs. When you die, I'll have you taxidermied. Then I will have you forever. I will spend the light of morning and the despair of midday and the lunatic peace of evening with you. Never will you lie at rest in a royal tomb.

And that is how I became an absolutely meaningless thing and survived time.

ABOUT THE AUTHOR

 Bae Suah was born in Seoul in 1965. After majoring in chemistry as an undergrad, she became a writer at the relatively late age of twenty-eight. Her first short story, which she wrote while learning how to type on a word processor, was published in a literary magazine. Prior to that, she had never taken any creative writing or literature classes. *Highway with Green Apples*, published in Korean in 1995 and then in the *Day One* journal in

December 2013 in English, is one of her first works. She continued to publish over the years, and in 2001 she moved to Berlin, where she took a break from writing to learn German. In 2008, she began translating German literature into Korean, beginning with Martin Walser's *Angstblute*. She has also translated two works by W. G. Sebald, one of her favorite German writers (*Nach der Natur* and *Schwindel. Gefuehle*, both forthcoming). She is a fan of the Portuguese writer Fernando Pessoa and has translated *The Book of Disquiet*.

ABOUT THE
TRANSLATOR

Sora Kim-Russell is a literary translator based in Seoul. Her translations include Shin Kyung-sook's *I'll Be Right There* and Gong Ji-young's *Our Happy Time*, as well as Bae Suah's *Highway with Green Apples*. She teaches at Ewha Womans University.

Printed in Great Britain
by Amazon